Karl Heinz Landenberger

Churchill's Mauser C96

Notes on

"The blow-up in Sydney Street"

from the London Decamerone

Produced and published by:
BoD – Books on Demand, Norderstedt
Copyright: 2019 Karl Heinz Landenberger
ISBN 978-3-7460-0930-8

1. Regional History Association

In Oberndorf, we have a very active regional history association with more than 100 members. During their events, almost every member actively contributes something personal, either from their own memory or that of their family and relatives. While the town is small, it has an interesting history. However, I often get the impression that even long-established Oberndorf residents know far too little about it. Therefore, during one of the association's meetings, I too wanted to make a small contribution by reading a story from a collection of London short stories, where weapons from the Mauser factory in Oberndorf play a leading role, and which are therefore related to Oberndorf's history.

2. Churchill's Pistol

For example, very few people know that Winston Churchill carried a Mauser C96 on him. He had received it as a birthday gift from his mother when he came of age. She must have been an exceptionally progressive woman, as she gave her son the absolute latest for those times, a world's first and top-of-the-range sensation – the first automatic weapon to arrive on the market – and that was back in 1896. Hence the name C96. However, it wasn't referred to known as "automatic" back then, but rather "self-loading".

3. English Imperialism

Already two years later, in 1898, the young, now 23-year old, Winston used this weapon. England was preparing to take back the colony of Sudan on the upper Nile, which had been lost eight years previously during the Mahdi Uprising.

The government did not risk this step until an English arms manufacturer had picked up on the Mauser 96 to develop weapons, which, while not yet "self-loading" like this Oberndorf precision weapon, were still semi-automatic. The Mahdists had a cavalry army of 60,000 warriors on horses and camels. The British would not have been able to risk this battle with their conventional weapons, but with this new kind of assault weapon, British expeditionary forces of 8,000 men managed to come out on top in the Battle of Omdurman, at the confluence of the White and Blue Niles. It was the last major cavalry battle in human history. 60,000 Sudanese soldiers with all their horses and camels were slaughtered without mercy.

4. River War

Churchill, as a young journalist, captured these events in a book entitled "River War". He also wrote reports to the largest English daily newspaper every day. He accompanied this campaign as a journalist. As his mother was politically very influential, she had managed to have him released from military service. As a result, he was able to travel with the English army as a private individual at his own expense. He also fought with them very privately thanks to his C96 and was very proud to have shot many insurgents.

5. From Cairo to Cape Town

However, his journey did not end with the victorious celebration in Khartoum. He wanted to travel via Northern and Southern Rhodesia, today known as Zimbabwe, to visit their namesake, Cecil Rhodes, who was now living in South Africa. There, the largest gold reserves in the world had been discovered in the Boer Republics of Transvaal and the Orange Free State. To this day. a third of the gold ever extracted in the world comes from there. Naturally, Cecil Rhodes did not want to pass up on this opportunity. However, the Boers, Dutch settlers, wanted to mine this gold in their countries themselves and did not grant Rhodes permission for extraction. This was clear discrimination against foreigners. For moral reasons, the British government could not, of course, condone this. So England declared war on the Boers.

6. The Boer Fight for Freedom

As uneducated farmers and cattle breeders could not, of course, contend with a regular army in an open battle, the farmers deferred to acts of sabotage at night. During the day, they hid themselves in well-known regions. In the end, the English Queen Victoria had to send 450,000 soldiers under General Kitchener to help the great adventurer Cecil Rhodes.

7. The best-paid journalist in the world

Churchill was among the party and fought with them fiercely. He even ended up being captured, where he succeeded in making a spectacular escape. He wrote that he had left a letter behind to "Ohm Krüger", the legendary leader of the Boers in his cell, where he apologized for fleeing his prison without asking for permission. In newspaper reports, he dressed up this escape in such a sensational way that everyone believed every word he wrote, leading to him being celebrated as **the hero** of the Boer Wars. At the age of 25, he was the best-paid journalist in the world, with a payment of one pound per line. While on the run, his C96 had often saved his life whenever he had to cross through areas where predators and lions roamed freely.

8.   Made in Germany

The high regard Churchill had for his Mauser is all the more remarkable as there could not possibly be anyone who hated German people more than he did. It was even impossible for him just to utter the word "German". For him, the Germans were simply "huns" or "beasts". They were competition for the English industry. Initially, the English had been pioneers of industrialization. First, they had invented the steam engine and the first locomotive. But the Germans soon overtook them. To ensure that none of the English bought products from Germans, each article produced in Germany had to be marked with "Made in Germany", clearly in English so that English consumers could understand it. If this label was missing, no items from Germany could be sent to England.

However, what was seen as a boycott soon developed into the opposite. Because German products were of such high quality, English housewives looked out for the quality mark "Made in Germany". The fact that Churchill therefore stuck with his "Made in Oberndorf" C96 his whole life remains astounding.

9. Source of the story "The Blow-Up in Sydney Street"

Following these initial remarks, I wanted to gradually come to reading the story from the London Decamerone. But first, I wanted to state where I found this story. It was actually a matter of coincidence. In London, the rooms where Churchill holed up during the Second World War, and from where he directed the war's events, have now been opened to visitors. These are known as the "War Rooms". It is a simple term, compared with Hitler's counter terms, "Führer Hauptquartier" (Leader's Headquarters) and "Wolfsschanze" (The Wolf's Lair). Churchill's rooms are located opposite Big Ben and Westminster Parliament, in the Treasury. The entrance is at the back of St James's Park. From there, you can see as far as Buckingham Palace. For protection against the bombs of the German air raids, it was sufficient to place a 3-meter thick layer of reinforced concrete between the ground floor and the first basement level. The rooms for Churchill and his war cabinet were located further below these; they included the private rooms: a small kitchen where only his meals were prepared, a small bedroom with one bed (his wife Clementine had to stay in their private home in Chartwell). And the card room, etc. One especially important room was the highly secret Transatlantic Telephone Room, disguised as a toilet, with a direct hotline to Franklin Roosevelt.

10. Churchill's Line of Life

These official and private rooms are connected to a small museum, which features a unique installation. If I remember correctly, it is called "Line of Life". A 15-meter long, horseshoe-shaped table with a touchscreen records all the press documents that can be found on Churchill from around the world, every day from the day he was born to the day he died. That is 90 years, each with 365 days, in the form of handwriting, photos, films and more. One "touch" with the fingers on a specific date projects all existing documents for that specific day onto a large screen. I don't think that such an effort has ever been made for anybody else in this world. Mere months would not be enough to call up even a small part of the material.

It was there that I found several stories from the London Decamerone. By chance, one of these was "The Blow-up in Sydney Street". It was, it seems, the last newspaper report after a long press battle - the swan song, so to speak. As a result, it was established that things had not been all that bad, just much ado about nothing. Two harmless crooks had simply attempted a jewelry robbery. There had been no terrorist background. The entire fuss had been for nothing. It was the final judgment of the mainstream press.

11. Decamerone

I also wanted to briefly explain the title of the London stories. Deca means 10. In his frame story, Boccaccio, who compiled his Decamerone in around 1300, lets 10 young nobles from Florence escape because the plague has broken out and they want to save themselves from this epidemic. Together, they go to a country estate outside of the city, one which belongs to them, and avoid any contact with other people. To make sure they don't get bored, they decide that every day each one of them will tell a story. They are there for 10 days. There are thus 10 stories 10 times. These are novellas, or news, as the author calls them, which everyone contributes as entertainment and pastime. The London stories are also arranged over 10 days and told by 10 different people. However, they do not feature such geometric regularity: one person tells many stories, another one fewer. Volume 1 covers the first five days. Volume 2 contains days six to eight. The 3rd volume does not appear until the next year, and then contains the stories from the ninth and tenth days.

12. The Reading

Here is the text of the story read out:

blow up

We opened the archive to a smaller story. To The Blow-Up in Sydney Street. At that time, Churchill was the Home Secretary and his ministry was not located far from Sydney Street. When he heard shots there, he ran immediately to where they were coming from. He couldn't be stopped when it came to shoot-outs, he had to join in.

Mauser

His mother had gifted him a Mauser for his 18th birthday. A wise gift for a young man. It would be nice if German mothers could also adopt this custom. Churchill always had the pistol on his person, his whole life long, and he had so many memories of the enemies he had shot with it that he didn't want to exchange it, even when an improved version arrived on the market.

The original model has become a cult weapon and can be bought from various weapons factories. It is priced at between 99 and 300 dollars.

Sydney Street

On this street, two intruders had broken into a jewelry shop and fired shots. When the house was surrounded by police, at which Churchill, standing on the street, fired back and the two crooks finally realized that they had no chance of escape. So they started a fire, hoping to perhaps escape amid the chaos of ambulances and firefighters. Churchill, who was the Home Secretary back then, forbade the fire department from extinguishing the fire in the house and it was left to burn down to its foundations. Entering the rubble, the two crooks were found in the lowest basement, sitting huddled together, totally burnt to a cinder.

Fire Rider

Perhaps someone knows the Mörike poem, "the Fire Rider". He leans on his horse towards the wall until he touches it. Then he says "Hush, it's falling into ashes." Such was the case with these two. Even as Churchill gave the order to have the two transported away to the Chamber of Horrors as a warning not to set fire to a house while you yourself were in it, they disintegrated into ashes. There was nothing left but to sweep the two bandits up with a broom.

Criticism

Churchill's role as the Home Secretary in this action has been heavily criticized.
On the one hand, people don't just start shooting so easily and secondly, a fire has to be extinguished. Even bandits can't just be allowed to burn to death.

Churchill responded to this as being all slander, that he had not even been present at this robbery. He had first heard about it in the newspaper.

However, as there were already cameras at that time, and Churchill could be seen in the front row of a photo published by one newspaper, he corrected himself and said, "But obviously, a home secretary has to be present on the front line in the event of such a criminal act."

All-Clear Signal

If a terrorist background had originally been assumed with this robbery, the all-clear signal was soon given. The two thieves had been entirely normal crooks. The huge fuss was literally for nothing.

13. Listeners' Reaction

As I understand it, after a story has been read out, it should be followed by a discussion about the material that has been read. Or at the very least, questions should be asked concerning passages that are incorrect or have only been half understood. That didn't happen. The older generation contented themselves, as was usual before, with passive listening, interrupted by at most an approving laugh or a nod of the head.

14. Explanations

So I added other interpretational remarks to this. First, on the title "Blow-up". Officially, it is known everywhere as the "Sidney Street Siege" or even "The Battle of Stepney". Stepney is the name of the London district where Sydney Street is located. Thus, translators also carried over the title. I myself have to admit that I hadn't thought any further, but rather that I had just carried over the heading of the newspaper article, as I had by coincidence tapped on the touchscreen of the Line of Life. By chance, it was the last publication in a week-long media circus. It was to be the final report that portrayed that everything had just been a "blow-up", that is, "blown out of proportion, excessively exaggerated". What was called a "blow-up" in 1911 would today be referred to as a huge hype. The Mainstreet Press therefore readjusted what more excited journalists had depicted as a subversive attack with roots in terrorism.
I think there are parallels to that today.

15. Digital Age

The digital age has now begun and I welcome that, because it is opening up opportunities today that were beyond imagination a few years ago. As such, thanks to email, Whatsapp, Twitter, Facebook and the rest, I have received messages from acquaintances that had read the London Decamerone and quickly expressed their opinion on it. They would certainly not have taken the time for a letter or a telephone call.

16. Wrong Date

Very briefly here. One friend corrected me in that Churchill did not receive the pistol for his 18th birthday. Today, people come of age when they are 18, but back then, it was at the age of 21. As the name C96 documents, the weapon arrived on the market in 1896. At that time, however, Churchill was 21 already.

17. Other Corrections

This was joined by a range of other corrections. I was delighted to receive each one, as it showed that people had read attentively. Every correction enhances the text. That's why in Part 2 of the London stories I wrote an interim balance as a preface, including several reader letters. As these short stories do not constitute scientific, historic research work, but rather a literary work, the "poetic freedom" excuses any deviation and fantastical embellishment.

18. Nameless Crooks

I would like to go into greater detail with a specific note from an acquaintance, specifically concerning the story I've just read. The events on Sydney Street were in no way just a blown-up press battle. The two burnt bodies in the basement of house 100 on Sydney Street were in no way nameless, but rather members of the notorious Piatkov Gang and probably known by name for years. It was the ashes of Fritz Schwarz and Josef Sokolow that had to be swept up with a broom.

19. The Piatkov Gang

This was a group of Latvian anarchists who in the period from 1905 to 1907 wanted to instigate a revolution and murder the Tsar in St. Petersburg, at that time the capital of Russia and seat of the Tsar in the Winter Palace. But neither assassination attempts nor riots proved successful. As a result, they finally had to flee and came to London as refugees when the Tsar finally asserted himself on 06/16/1907.

20. Why London?

Well, that's very easy. The English Secret Service had trained these anarchists, provided them with weapons training for the riot and sent them with money to St. Petersburg. England wanted to weaken the Tsarist empire, or better, to abolish it. At the same time, the Japanese in the Far East had incited a war against Russia and were so richly outfitted with weapons and finances that the Tsar had to accept a catastrophic defeat there and lost his entire Pacific fleet.

21. Lenin and Stalin

Other groups also came to London: anarchists, communists, social revolutionaries - because they could hope for support in London. Even Lenin and Stalin spent a long time in London. It is no secret that Marx spent his last years of life in London and there wrote his main work "Das Kapital". London was the hub of international communism. It is suspected that the Comintern headquarters paid to maintain Marx and his large family for years. This center was sponsored by influential freemasons, such as Baron von Rothschild.

22. Violent Robberies

However, it is also a fact that the revolutionaries were dissatisfied with the amount of money allocated to them. As activists for the classless society, it was nevertheless not difficult for them to enforce their mottos in their host country and that meant expropriation of the expropriators, meaning they committed violent robberies, because "property is theft", and owners must be ousted as a result.

23. Tottenham

One of the most spectacular robberies took place on 01/23/1909 in Tottenham. There, they robbed a money emissary that was fetching wages from the bank. After pursuing the perpetrators over several miles, two were left dead and 27 injured.

24. Houndsditch

Here, they rented an apartment directly next to a jewelry shop. They knocked a hole through the wall in order to reach the adjoining building. The police were alerted to the noise caused by knocking through the stone wall. The first policeman that arrived on the scene was shot dead immediately. A second met the same fate in the ensuing shootout. The members of the gang, however, were all able to evade capture by the police. They all had a Mauser C96.

25. Outrage

The outrage over the two police murders was so great among the population that a manhunt was launched. Several members of the gang were arrested, but then they all had to be released again because it could not be clarified beyond a doubt which pistols had fired the fatal shots at the policemen.

26. Act of State

The two killed policemen were honored in an official act of state, which the Home Secretary and Chief of the Secret Police Sir Winston Churchill personally attended. He even brought his wife Clementine with him.

27. The Sidney Street Siege

These events all preceded the incident on Sidney Street. The Home Secretary Churchill, responsible for security, therefore, knew exactly who was involved when he was notified that the Piatkov Gang had holed up at 100 Sidney Street.

28. List of Names

The militant core of the troupe were: Jakob Vogel as well as Hans Sprohe actively, then Josef Sokolov, Fritz Schwarz, Georg Gardstein, Luba Milstein, Jakob Peters, Max Schmoller – also known as Josef Lewi – and the most important, Peter Piatkov. As they all had several identities, known as "alibis" back then, the precise size of the gang could not be determined.

29. Beginning of the Action

On 01/03/1911, at 2:00 in the morning, 200 police officers surrounded the housing block. Shots began to be exchanged at 6:00 in the morning. The bandits all had the Mauser C96, and the engagement advantage of those trapped over the English police quickly became clear. The bandits continued to shoot with their "self-loading" pistols, while the British had to reload after every shot. The officer-in-charge soon requested the support of the military. The special troops of the Scots Guards stationed in the Tower arrived to help but even these did not succeed in storming the building.

30. Fire

Around noon/lunchtime, a fire broke out in the upper floors and slowly spread downstairs. Churchill, who was then leading the operation, forbade the firefighting forces that were arriving from putting out the fire. They were only allowed to prevent the fire from spreading to the adjacent building. They waited patiently until the fire reached the ground floor, upon which the roof collapsed.

31. Criticism

The role that Churchill played here confirmed his reputation as a scandal-ridden minister in public opinion. Balfour, Head of the Conservative Party, accused him of having acted in a way unbefitting of a minister due to his personal involvement in a gunfight, especially in front of the live cameras of the British weekly newsreel.

32. Balfour Declaration

Balfour succeeded in moving the USA to enter the war against Germany with his Balfour declaration. After 300,000 had fallen in the Battle of the Somme and England had practically been defeated, he promised Bernard Baruch that if the USA would declare war on the German emperor, he would in return provide the Jews in Palestine with the Holy Land to form their Jewish State.

This was an astounding promise, as Palestine did not actually belong to the British. It was part of the Ottoman Empire and would first have to be wrested from the Turkish Sultan. Three days after the agreement with Baruch, the first English war ships landed in Jaffa to take the country by force.

33. New Weapons for the London Police

The clear disadvantage of the traditional English weapons triggered a complete rearmament of the London Police. Of course, the weapons were not purchased from Mauser — English pride would not allow it. Instead, the weapons manufacturer Wembley built a semi-automatic weapon based on the German model as a standard weapon for the London Police.

34. New Deployment

However, it seems that in this large-scale operation far more of the bandits died than the two physical remains found. Many survived, however, and towards the end of the First World War the English secret service was able to travel by sea to St. Petersburg, freshly armed and equipped with finances, where they supported Lenin and Stalin in the October Revolution.

35. Why was the fire not extinguished?

Why did Churchill prevent the fire from being put out? First and foremost, it probably had to do with the fact that it was the easiest way to eliminate the bandits. As the Home Secretary and Chief of the Secret Police, he knew them by name. A trial against them would have posed major problems for the British judicial system because they were members of the British secret service. On the other hand, the fire was of course beneficial in eliminating any forensic evidence. House No. 100 had long been the headquarters of the gang. The gang's collaboration with the English Secret Service would not have been accepted by large sections of the English people.

36. Later Success

Jakob Peters, a member of the Piatkov gang, had obviously succeeded in breaking out during the Sydney Street Siege, but had been acquitted along with his 5 codefendants because there was no evidence that he had been present at 100 Sydney Street at the time, became Chief of the Notorious Secret Police,

Cheka, in 1917. All the Bolsheviks stayed faithful to their Mauser C96. This weapon played a crucial role for them. It can safely be assumed that Lenin and Stalin also owned this weapon.

37. Mayakovsky

Mayakovsky was the great poet of the October Revolution. He commemorated the significance of this weapon in a poem:

> About turn, march!
> Away with a talk show,
> Silence, you speakers!
> You have the floor,
> speak, Comrade Mauser!

Anyone who isn't familiar with Mayakovsky's work should read his comedy "The Bedbug".

38. Fidel Feederle

In all the praise and global acclaim for the Mauser C96, however, one person is always forgotten, and that is the inventor of this sensational innovation in weapons technology. He was an engineer at Mauser. Even long-established Oberndorf residents do not know that this pistol should actually be called the Fidel Feederle. With the help of his two younger brothers, he developed this weapon with a magazine charge of 6/10/20 rounds.

39. Tombstone in the Talfriedhof cemetery

A street in Oberndorf has been named after him and the simple gravestone put up when he died in 1930 has not been removed.

40. His Son

When I came to Oberndorf in 1970, his son was Vice Principal of a school. In 1971, the Abitur was taken in Oberndorf for the first time and the Progymnasium become the Gymnasium am Rosenberg. Mr. Feederle was one of the most likeable colleagues. He did a lot of voluntary work in Oberndorf, He had managed the Oberndorf Local Museum for years, for example. Unfortunately, he did not live much longer after retiring. He was laid to rest in his father's grave. His name was merely added to the old gravestone.

41. Town History

It is the honorable task of the Local History Association to keep the memory of the history of the town and the people that shaped the town through their work and inventive spirit alive. I hope that I have helped a little through this contribution. Fidel Feederle is truly an international-level inventor, and that should not be forgotten.

42. Postscript

"The Sidney Street Siege" or "The Battle of Stepney", as it is known colloquially, still occupies many minds because people assume that Churchill wanted to conceal such a mean trick.

43. Film Adaption

In 1934, Alfred Hitchcock took the opportunity to make a film entitled "The Man Who Knew Too Much". In 1956, he even remade the material.
Monty Berman filmed the 1960 feature "The Siege of Sidney Street".

44. Books

In 1981, a book was released by Colin Rogers in London, entitled The Battle of Stepney: The Sidney Street Siege, its Causes and Consequences.
Donald Rumbelow published a book in 1988: The Houndsditch Murders and The Siege of Sidney Street.
From this, we can see that the Londoners were not content with the obvious cover-up of this affair.

45. Final Remark

This "tolerance" and "protection" of criminals whenever they commit an offense in their host country is reminiscent of today's circumstances. Syrian "Freedom Fighters" that have fought against Assad receive a preferential right of asylum here in Germany. They are considered victims of political persecution. If they have been complicit in murder and torture, they may face trial and possible sentencing on their return. For this reason, many Syrians commit crimes so that their stay in Germany is guaranteed. So far so good. Except that if they commit an offense in Germany, the judicial system has major problems because the public will demand sentencing, but German courts will not have the right to punish employees of the American CIA.